The FOOT BOOK

WITHDRAWN

By Dr. Seuss

HarperCollins *Children's Books*

17 19 20 18 16

ISBN : 978-0-00-717310-5

© 1968, 1996 by Dr. Seuss Enterprises, L.P.
All Rights Reserved
A Bright and Early Book for Beginning Beginners,
published by arrangement with Random House Inc.,
New York, USA
First published in the UK 1969
This edition published in the UK 2004 by
HarperCollins*Children's Books*,
a division of HarperCollins*Publishers* Ltd
77-85 Fulham Palace Road
London W6 8JB

Visit our website at:
www.harpercollins.co.uk

Printed and bound in Hong Kong

Left foot
Left foot

Right foot
Right

Feet in the morning

Feet at night

Left foot

Left foot

Left foot

Right

Wet foot

Dry foot

High foot

Low foot

Front feet

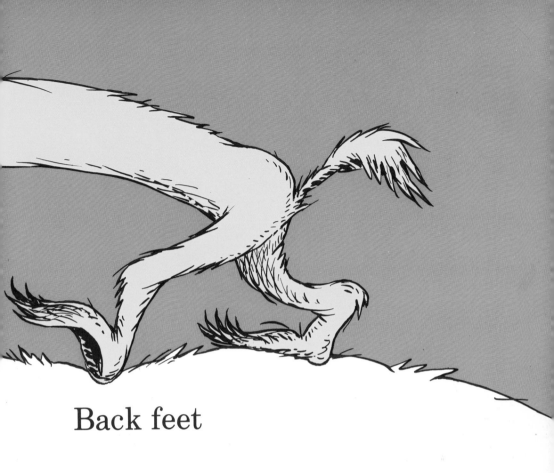

Back feet

Red feet

Black feet

Left foot   Right foot

Feet   Feet   Feet

How many, many
feet you meet.

Slow feet

Quick feet

Trick feet

Sick feet

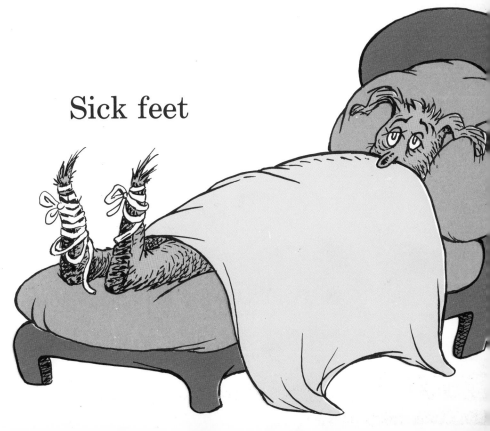

Up feet

Down feet

Here come clown feet.

Small feet

Big feet

Here come pig feet.

His feet

Her feet

Fuzzy fur feet

In the house,
and on the street,

how many, many
feet you meet.

Up in the air feet

Over a chair feet

More and more feet

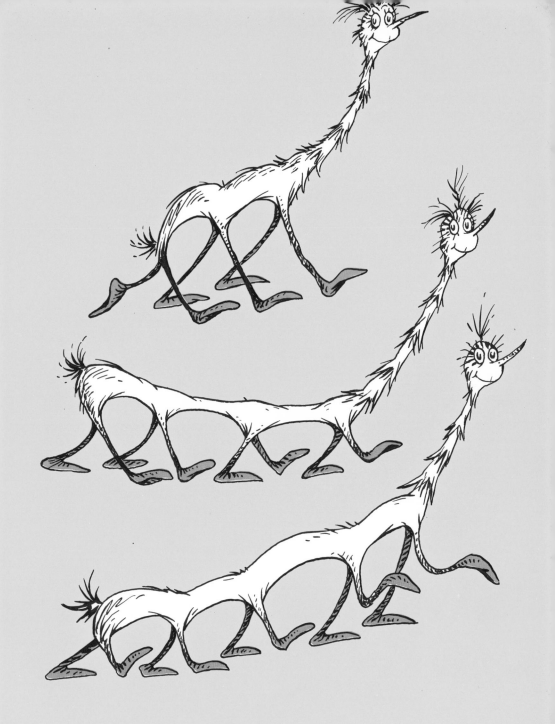

Twenty-four feet

Here come
more and more . . . .

. . . . and more feet!

Left foot.   Right foot.

Feet. Feet. Feet.

Oh, how many
feet you meet!

Read them **together**, read them **alone**, read them **aloud** and make **reading fun!** With over **50 wacky** stories to choose from, now it's **easier** than **ever** to find the right **Dr. Seuss** books for your child – just let the **back cover colour** guide you!

Here's a great selection to choose from:

Blue back books
for sharing with your child

Dr. Seuss's ABC
A Fly Went By
The Bears' Picnic
The Bike Lesson
The Eye Book
The Foot Book
Go, Dog, Go!
Hop on Pop
I'll Teach My Dog 100 Words
Inside Outside Upside Down
Mr. Brown Can Moo! Can You?
One Fish, Two Fish, Red Fish, Blue Fish
The Shape of Me and Other Stuff
There's a Wocket in my Pocket!

Green back books
for children just beginning to read on their own

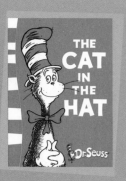

A Fish Out of Water
And to Think That I Saw It on Mulberry Street
Are You My Mother?
The Bears' Holiday
Bears On Wheels
The Best Nest
The Cat in the Hat
The Cat in the Hat Comes Back
Come Over To My House
The Digging-est Dog
Fox in Socks
Gerald McBoing Boing
Green Eggs and Ham
Happy Birthday to YOU
Hunches in Bunches
I Can Read With My Eyes Shut!
I Wish That I Had Duck Feet
Marvin K. Mooney Will You Please Go Now!
Oh, Say Can You Say?
Oh, the Thinks You Can Think!
Ten Apples Up on Top
Wacky Wednesday

Yellow back books
for fluent readers to enjoy

The 500 Hats of Bartholomew Cubbins
Daisy-Head Mayzie
Did I Ever Tell You How Lucky You Are?
Dr. Seuss's Sleep Book
Horton Hatches the Egg
Horton Hears a Who!
How the Grinch Stole Christmas!
If I Ran the Circus
If I Ran the Zoo
I Had Trouble in Getting to Solla Sollew
The Lorax
McElligot's Pool
Oh, the Places You'll Go!
On Beyond Zebra
Scrambled Eggs Super!
The Sneetches and other stories
Thidwick the Big-Hearted Moose
Yertle the Turtle and other stories